Gem N Me
Penny Publishing Co.
United Black Fund

All rights reserved. No part of this book may be reproduced in any manner what so ever with out written permission.

6 Little Descendants

Written By Arie Shorter

Descendants

My name is Molly, and my favorite color is blue. Even, if I'm wearing a shirt that say "I love pink." I have two curly ponytails, and I'm the youngest of 3 children. I have one older sister and an older brother. The last thing you should know is that I have a book of spells under my bed that my grandma gave to me.

I'm Ci Ci, I am Molly's older sister. I am fun, loving, and have a dark side. What exactly is a dark side? It's when a person has a devious personality, but I only shows at home. Like, the mystery of who put dirt on the couch. "I didn't frame my brother and got him grounded"," says CiCi sarcastically, slowly laughing. I got a magic crystal ball from my grandma. Molly thinks it's dumb, but it's just because she doesn't know my grandma like I do. But I do have a different grandma than her.

Mily is five seconds older than Lily. "Yeah, and she always acts like the boss!" said Lily. "Hey! Stay out. I am the boss!".!". I am also an animal lover and a protest queen." We wear our hair with one bun at the top and curls at the bottom. We got a twin alternator from our grandmother, which is a tool that we use to make potions from our minds. We can even do it lying down! The only thing is that we both have to work together.

My younger twin Lily loves bright colors, and she has a whole collection of sweatshirts that have good vibes on them. She doesn't like when I wear them without permission. Everything else about us is pretty much the same.

Cindy believes in myths like unicorns, trolls, and dragons. Her favorite color is light pink, and she is very specific about most things in her life. "My grandma gave me a scepter that has missing gem holders. I'm an only child, and my mom lets me do anything to my hair. She even lets me dye it light pink"," said Cindy.

Water is the only child in her family and has a best friend named Molly. "I wear jumpsuits all the time in Aventown. I have natural hair, and I have two grandmothers that were magical. One was in the Descendants club, and one was not, but I got the first gem they found in a magical cube.

Chapter 1

The people in Aventown kept debating if the 6 girls had powers or not. People kept saying that the strange things happening was just a coincidence. One day the group of girls had a school assignment to finish in the library. After they were done, they tried to get to the bottom of the powers and magic stuff, but they didn't quite understand.

While the girls were in the library, they were talking about magic and spells. Then suddenly, books came flying off of the shelves and landed right in front of them. Water picked up a book which opened up to a page with a magical cube. The page told Water to only tell her best friend the power that she had because she could not trust everyone.

The book told the girls that they had to complete all of the adventures together so that they could find all of the spells, cubes, and gems. After they completed all of the adventures, the girls would learn something new about each of their grandmothers and themselves.

Molly screamed and ran out. "Molly, it's ok!" said Water. My grandma told me that this would happen. My grandma told me this story when I was young, and I just remembered it.

My grandma said that the first person you should tell your power to is your best friend. We all have a special power, but we still need to learn what it is and how to use it through all of us using the book. While we are on the adventure, we will find all the spells, the cube, and the gems. We will learn more and see more.

My grandma said she would help us with our magic, and each of the girls will see more of their grandma. She also said one girl would practice black magic, but we will have to wait until we go to the mountain to see who it is. This doesn't mean this girl is bad; it's just that she acts like her grandma-which means being jealous. Don't listen to all that the stupid book says cause some of it is not true. Oh! One more thing- we all have a souvenir from our grandmother. The girls decided to check the book out of the library so that they could complete the tasks.

Chapter Two

The first page of the Magic Spellbook talks about the cube, which none of the girls knew about except for Water.

"Hey, we found the cube on the first page," said Lily.

"Ok, but who told you guys?" said Cindy.

"We just read it in the book," said the other girls.

"Wow, that's cool. So we found where the cube is located. It's at the top of the mountain. We'll do it tomorrow. Come on, Molly," said Ci Ci. Because they are sisters. Lily and Mily are twin sisters and Cindy and Water are best friends.

The next day the group of girls looked in the magic book together. The book told the girls how and where to find the 5 missing gems.

When the girls find the 5 missing gems, they have to go to the mountain top, put the gems back in their place, and then the journey will be complete when the yellow beam is coming out of the mountaintop. The book warns the group not to let the dark magic girl get to the mountain top first so that she doesn't do bad things with the powers. Cindy started joking around that since Ci Ci is the meanest, she is probably the dark girl!

Ci Ci started singing to distract the girls, and then Ci Ci's voice flew Cindy to the roof, and Ci Ci said, "Ha!!! Who's the meanest now?" Then Ci Ci dropped Cindy, but she landed on a pile of books. When the girls saw that, they said, "That's your power! Super strength voice! You can lift heavy items by singing." The girls agreed to start the adventure the next day.

Chapter Three

While the other girls were hanging out without Ci Ci. Water said, "stop Ci Ci from getting the gem." Molly said, "Ci Ci is not evil. She's my sister even though she may be a little mean sometimes." "But your sister got black magic!" said Water. "Prove it," exclaimed Molly. "Ok! During sleepover at your place tonight, I'm going to prove it," said Water. Later that night, the girls came over and made Ci Ci mad again because Molly stole her crystal ball. Milly found her power, solving from puzzles at Molly and Ci Ci's house. The girls found the coin slot in Ci Ci's crystal ball and decided to put a coin in it.

The crystal ball started to talk, BUT the crystal ball only thought Ci Ci was there, not all of the girls. "Finally, you took me out. Now we can destroy the Descendants. I am the one with Black magic, and you are too. Make sure you get all of the crystals before the girls do so you have the power to make everyone in Aventown your slaves. If the girls get the crystals first, they will have the power."

Ci Ci tries to get the ball back from the girls and threatens to break Molly's stuff. Water said, "I told you."

The girls started looking at the book to see what gem they needed next. Water grabbed the cube since that is what the book said. The girls have to figure out how to solve the cube because the next gem is stuck inside. Milly solved the cube in only 2 minutes because that was her power. The crystal was so hot they dropped it, and it exploded on the ceiling with clues to find the other crystals.

1st clue - Take the magic test in the book from the library.

2nd clue - On page 34 of the book, they looked at the book, and there was a test that had 3 questions. The first question was, "How many gems were to be found altogether?"

Lilly answered, "5 more gems to go." The book beamed 'correct' on the ceiling. The 2nd question was for Cindy — "Where do you put all 6 crystals when you are done?" - Cindy answered, "In the mountain that will beam yellow." The book beamed on the ceiling again, 'correct.'

The 3rd question was for Ci Ci - Cici was still mad at the other girls, so they had to trick her to get the answer. The girls also did not want to include her because she was practicing dark magic, and they did not want to take her to the mountain top.

Molly found out a deep secret of Ci Ci's and told Ci Ci that if she didn't tell the girls the answer to the question, she would tell mom the secret. So Ci Ci agreed to answer the question. The last question — "Where do you find the mountain on the map? Ci Ci figured out they were doing the quest without her. So the crystal ball beam 'denied' so that the girls would have to try again tomorrow.

The girls went to sleep since they could not finish the quest, and they woke up the next morning.

Chapter Four

The next day, Ci Ci went to the crystal ball, and the crystal ball said, "I knew it wasn't you. You can't rush the adventure. It has to be a 5-day process."

Ci Ci stole the book from the girls.

"Ci Ci put it down!" said Molly. "Why do you want to make me mad? You know I have powers and a temper," said Ci Ci. "And I know you stole my crystal ball when your friends were over last night. We are going to have a magic war when they leave," said Ci Ci with a lot of sass. Molly went back to her friends. "You guys were right. She said she knows we have her crystal ball. And when you guys leave, we are going to have a magic war. So can you get me ready?" "Yes, I guess. You can use our potion," said the twins. "What is it?" "It's a sleep spell.

We put it on our parents, and it makes them sleep for an extra hour, or we can use Mily's power which is problem-solving. We are going to use Mily's power as a test. We will see how she can defend herself with her powers."

Chapter Five

All of the girls started to experiment to find their powers, especially Molly, so her sister wouldn't destroy her in the magic battle. The girls tried to morph objects, fly and see if they had x-ray vision. "What happens if she beats me in the magic battle?" said Molly. Then Water answered, "Your power will be lost forever since you're fighting against black magic." "How do you know that?" said Milly. Water said, "I just looked it up in the book." "I found my power last night," said Milly. "Way to go," said Lilly.

"So with Milly's problem solving and with Water's super memory, we got this. Now we just have to find Lilly, Molly, and Cindy's powers." "Easy peasy lemon squeezy," said Milly. "What does that even mean?" said Cindy. "I heard it in a phrasebook, ok." "Let's get my scepter from my house," said Cindy. "But we're at Molly's house. "Does somebody have transportation power?"

"But your house is two miles away! We will have to practice with something easy and light," said Molly. "Ok, we can save that for later tonight. Let's see who has teleportation powers." The girls took turns calling the book to get it to come to them. It worked for Cindy. Cindy can teleport objects to her or send them to another place. Let's just look in the book for the fifth and sixth power. The girls started to look through the book for what the other girls' powers were.

Lilly's power is levitating! Molly's power is turning things invisible. At the bottom of the book, it says to look in the level up chapter to level up powers.

"Ok, before we do anything, we have to train Molly." "Yay! and we don't even have to wait for the morning to see if somebody has transportation powers."

The girls started to practice for the magic war. Molly and Water practiced first. "Ready, set, go!" Water did a spell called 'sleep sleep for a beat' which made Molly sleep for a minute then wake her up with really loud music. The book kept track of who won each round automatically. It goes down in the magic book that Water won her first battle.

Then the book flipped to a new chapter beginning with Water, and it said 'level two witch power.' But don't worry, since they are friends, nothing will happen to Molly unless she is beaten three times in a row. "I know how to get Molly ready, practice making objects invisible, and then move them." "I did it!" said Molly. That's good, or instead of doing the battle, we can say we found our first clue to the second gem. Go get your gem out of the bag. We need to look at which gem is a color blast punch or a color spin twirl. It is actually the last gem, not the first one. That means we have to use the scepter to show us the first gem.

All of the girls went to sleep but Ci Ci was talking to her grandmother in the crystal ball. Ci Ci told her grandmother that other girls know she practices black magic and the grandma start changing her plans. Grandma told Ci Ci that she should complete the entire quest tonight while the others are sleeping so she could be the first to get to the mountains. Before grandma left she said to make sure the other girls don't get the last gem and put it in the scepter. "Nothing will stop us".

Chapter Six

The next morning, the book beamed on the wall. It said if you have the last gems but not the first gem, then get a scepter and put the gem on top of it, and the other gems will form in the next 24 hours. To erase this off your wall, just read it out loud. We got dressed and went over to Water's house and got the scepter, and the gem started to glow. When we tried to leave the house, it wouldn't let us. Now, what we're going to do? Oh, I remember that every witch at least can make one spell. How about I make an invisible shield over the house, so nobody sees it growing and lifting. "Wait, it's floating," Water said.

Hey, but what are we going to do? Let's look for the map to get to the mountain? Ok, let's just set up the test in the book so we can get the map from the book. Are you ready for the map test? "Yes," said the girls. What are the two animals in the mountain? Water guessed, "I think unicorn pegasus and tigerbear." You are partially right! I'll give you a hint. Some people say they see this mythical animal. "Oh, phoenix." "Four more questions to go. This one is for lily," said the book. "Where do you put the gems?" Lily said, "The circle thing in the mountain."

"Yes, this one is for Molly. What happens if you lose a magic battle three times in a row?" "You lose your powers forever." "Here's the last question; this one is for Milly. What happens if Ci Ci beats you there?" "She takes over and makes everybody her slave."

"Cindy, but let me give you a chance. How many real descendants are there in a group?" "Five." "Yep, now you all made it. Here is the map." "Thank you. Now we've got twenty more hours to go. Let's go to sleep, ok, goodnight." They woke up, and it said two hours left. So they made breakfast and washed up, and it was time to hit the road. They went outside. "Since we got all five, let's go to the mountain." "Let's fly," said Lily and Cindy because they could fly, and the twins could make flying positions. "Shouldn't we practice first?" "No, it's fine, it should be ok.

Chapter Seven

So how do we get off the ground by jumping?" said Water. "Ok, now lead the way," said Cindy to Molly. Because you got the book, we got a long journey. It says if you fly, it will be 5 hours with the challenges. "What challenges," said the twins. Like the mean Phoenixes or the unicorn Pegasus, which is a unicorn and a Pegasus put together. The last one is the hardest. It's all your fears put together. So that's five fears altogether.

Yay, we made it through the Phoenixes, unicorn pegasus, and fear. Now we go to put the gem in the mountain. We did it, and the mountain said, "Now you guys all have level twenty powers." When the girls put the gems in the mountain, Ci Ci no longer knew or had power.
And now it's actually five descendants!

The End

Made in the USA
Middletown, DE
29 July 2022